SACRED MUSIC
FROM THE
LAMBETH CHOIRBOOK

RECENT RESEARCHES IN THE MUSIC OF THE RENAISSANCE

James Haar, general editor

A-R Editions, Inc., publishes six quarterly series—

Recent Researches in the Music of the Middle Ages and Early Renaissance
Margaret Bent, general editor

Recent Researches in the Music of the Renaissance
James Haar, general editor

Recent Researches in the Music of the Baroque Era
Robert L. Marshall, general editor

Recent Researches in the Music of the Classical Era
Eugene K. Wolf, general editor

Recent Researches in the Music of the Nineteenth and Early Twentieth Centuries
Rufus Hallmark, general editor

Recent Researches in American Music
H. Wiley Hitchcock, general editor—

which make public music that is being brought to light
in the course of current musicological research.

Each volume in the *Recent Researches* is devoted
to works by a single composer or to a single genre of composition,
chosen because of its potential interest to scholars and performers,
and prepared for publication according to the standards that govern
the making of all reliable historical editions.

Subscribers to this series, as well as patrons of subscribing institutions,
are invited to apply for information about the "Copyright-Sharing Policy"
of A-R Editions, Inc., under which the contents of this volume
may be reproduced free of charge for study or performance.

Correspondence should be addressed:

A-R EDITIONS, INC.
315 West Gorham Street
Madison, Wisconsin 53703

RECENT RESEARCHES IN THE MUSIC OF THE RENAISSANCE • VOLUME LXIX

Robert Fayrfax

SACRED MUSIC FROM THE LAMBETH CHOIRBOOK

Edited by Margaret Lyon

A-R EDITIONS, INC. • MADISON

For

AUNT ROMOLA
in her hundredth year

&

For

SARAH, VALENTINA, ELIZABETH, and ZACHARY
in their first

Library of Congress Cataloging in Publication Data

Fayrfax, Robert, 1464–1521.
  [Vocal music.   Selections]
  Sacred music from the Lambeth Choirbook.

  (Recent researches in the music of the Renaissance,
0486–123X ; v. 69)
  Contents: Mass Regali ex progenie—Magnificat
"Regale"—Aeterne laudis lilium.
  1. Sacred vocal music.   I. Lyon, Margaret. prf.
II. Lambeth Palace Library.   Manuscript. MS 1.
III. Title.   IV. Series.
M2.R2384   vol. 69   [M3.1]   84–760380
ISBN 0–89579–150–1

Contents

Preface

In the years immediately following the Second World War, scholars in England and in this country turned to one of the remaining *lacunae* in the history of western music, the period in England that began with the death of Dunstable and extended throughout the early years of the Tudors, a span of some ninety years from 1453 to 1545. The pioneering work of Dom Anselm Hughes and the publication of the works of Robert Fayrfax by Edwin B. Warren focused on the principal composer at the court of Henry VII and the court of Henry VIII and made available for the first time the full spectrum of the music of this great English composer of the Renaissance.

The present publication of three sacred works by Robert Fayrfax is intended to draw attention once again to this most famous of the early Tudor composers and to the three principal forms of sacred music in the Renaissance as they were developed in England. It updates Hughes's and Warren's work in that it takes advantage of the normal progress of research and discovery that, in the course of the past twenty years and more, has added to our understanding of the period that saw the end of the Wars of the Roses and the establishment of the Tudors on the throne of England.

Haec eis Anglici nunc (licet vulgariter jubilare, Gallici vero cantare dicunter) veniunt conferendi. ("Nor can the English, who are popularly said to shout while the French sing, stand comparison with them.")[1] The Franco-Flemish theorist and composer Tinctoris (d. 1511?) wrote this ca. 1476 in the dedication to his *Proportionale musices*. He was quoting a saying current at the time to support his observation that, whereas the English, headed by Dunstable (d. 1453), had been the "fount and origin" of a new art of music, they had then continued to use the same style of composition, showing a "wretched poverty of invention," while the French were composing in the "newest manner for the new times." Dufay (d. 1474), in his late works, had brought the style of the Renaissance to its first great height of artistic expression. He had been succeeded by Ockeghem, Busnois, Regis, and Caron, the "moderns" whom Tinctoris greatly admired.

But while Tinctoris acknowledged the influence of the English on the Continental composer earlier in the century, he failed to appreciate the continuing vitality of the English of his generation. He recognized their reliance upon the past but did not see that they had developed and carried forward the great achievements of Dunstable and Power (d. 1445). Frank Ll. Harrison considers the culmination of this tradition to have been reached in the work of composers in the early Tudor period—a final manifestation of the medieval spirit that paralleled Perpendicular Gothic architecture in England. He states further that the transition from Gothic to Renaissance in England was not completed until the Latin ceremony, of which the florid style in English sacred music was an ornament, was abolished and replaced in 1549 by the English liturgy of the Reformation.[2] Harrison, therefore, includes the music of Fayrfax and Taverner (d. 1545) in his history, *Music in Medieval Britain*.[3] Gustave Reese, on the other hand, in the light of what he calls insular traits, considers Fayrfax (1464–1521) stylistically an early Renaissance figure, although he is a younger contemporary of the great Josquin (1440–1521).[4] At no time, it seems safe to say, does the music of England fit squarely the musical changes and emphases taking place on the Continent. Although English composers may lead, follow, or anticipate events in the mainstream, they always retain qualities that show the natural inclinations and musical taste of the English.

Neither the retention of an English sound and a predilection for highly developed forms and massive choral effects, nor the lack of contrapuntal devices and the profound expressiveness associated with Josquin should obscure the many aspects of English music at the turn of the fifteenth century that place it in the Renaissance. Although in Fayrfax's works the long melodic lines in florid, abstract counterpoint and the mid-century approach to formal concepts based upon a structural tenor cantus firmus and sections of counterpoint clearly defined by changes in texture and vocal range may have come directly from Dunstable and Power, the musical aesthetics, language, and effect belong to the Renaissance.

The Lambeth Choirbook (Lambeth Palace, MS 1) is one of the principal sources for sacred music in England between the time of Dunstable and that of Taverner (1453–1545). It is at the same time a primary source specifically for the music of Fayrfax, of whose music more has survived than that by any other composer of this important generation in England.

The Composer

The musical career of Robert Fayrfax coincided almost exactly with the reign of Henry VII (1485–1509) and with the first twelve years in that of Henry VIII. He served both kings as a member of the Chapel Royal, enjoying the favor of royalty over a long period of his life.

Fayrfax was born 23 April 1464 at Deeping Gate, Lincolnshire. He died 24 October 1521 at St. Albans, Hertfordshire, and was buried there in the abbey. The administration of his estate was granted to his wife, Agnes, on 14 November 1521. The exact date of his death, however, is known only from a sketch which was made in the seventeenth century of the monumental brass on his tomb. Some time later the brass was lost from the tomb.

His relation to St. Albans Abbey is not clear. His entombment there suggests that he held a post at the abbey. It has been generally supposed that he was *informator chori,* at least in 1502. Pulver and Grattan Flood indicate he was also organist.[5] Denis Stevens states further that Fayrfax accepted the post of *informator chori* as early as 1498 and that he lived and worked at St. Albans while retaining his place in the Chapel Royal until his death.[6] But most recently Sandon writes that it is unlikely that Fayrfax was ever employed at St. Albans, perhaps having had an "honorary association that required occasional composition of music."[7]

Fayrfax is first mentioned as a Gentleman of the King's Chapel on 6 December 1497 in the 1496–97 Calendar of Patent Rolls of Henry VII on the occasion of the grant of the free chapel in Snodhill Castle, Herefordshire, a chapelry which he relinquished the following year. (In this relation it should be noted that his Magnificat *"Regale,"* a mature work, can be dated as early as 1490.) On 23 February 1504 his name stands ninth in a list of eighteen Gentlemen of the Chapel Royal to whom liveries were issued for the funeral of Queen Elizabeth of York. Five years later, in 1509, his name heads this list for the funeral of Henry VII on 9 May and for the coronation of Henry VIII on 24 June. His name also heads the list of Gentlemen of the Chapel Royal receiving liveries for the funeral of Prince Henry, infant son of Henry VIII, on 27 February 1511. Throughout the remainder of his life Fayrfax was the chief member of the Chapel Royal, and in this capacity he accompanied King Henry in 1520 to his meeting with the French king at the Field of the Cloth of Gold.[8]

The esteem in which the composer was held by his royal patron is apparent in the honors bestowed upon him by the king and in a series of New Year's Day payments of unusually high amounts for music manuscripts. On 20 June 1509 he received from Henry VIII, on the eve of his coronation, a grant for life of £ 9 2s. 6d.

yearly. After 15 October 1513 he shared this with a certain Robert Bithesee. He held a corody, an allowance of provisions for maintenance, in the monastery of Stanley, which he surrendered in favor of a colleague on 21 February 1513. And as a special mark of royal favor he was created a Poor Knight of Windsor on 10 September 1514 with 12d. a day for life.

The first New Year's Day payment for music manuscripts is recorded in 1516, a reward of £ 13 6s. 8d. for a book. In 1517 he received £ 20 for a book of anthems, £ 20 for a "pricksongebook" in 1518, followed by £ 20 for a "balet-boke limned" in 1519.

Fayrfax earned three university degrees. He graduated with a Bachelor of Music from Cambridge in 1501 and with a Doctor of Music in 1504. According to a comment written in the Lambeth Choirbook (fol. 8v), his exercise for the doctorate was the Mass *O quam glorifica*.[9] In 1511 he was incorporated Doctor of Music at Oxford.

Of the extant music of his generation in England, that of Fayrfax exceeds any other composer. Twenty-nine of his works are known today. These include eight partsongs (one incomplete); three instrumental works (two puzzle canons and the bass of what was probably a hexachord fantasia); six cyclic masses (one incomplete); two Magnificats; and ten votive antiphons (five incomplete).[10] At least seven works are known to have been lost: a Magnificat, a Nunc Dimittis, three antiphons, one or more of seven sequences, and a partsong.

In the early Tudor period it was music for the church that primarily engaged the attention of the English composer and for which his talent and skill were in demand. Secular music in England, such as polyphonic carols and court songs —although by no means neglected—did not reach the same artistic level as that achieved in sacred music, nor, for that matter, that of the chanson on the Continent. Thus it is the sacred music for which Fayrfax, the chief member of the Chapel Royal, was known and for which he remains important today.

A number of sacred works can be dated. The two antiphons *Ave lumen gratiae* and *Salve regina* and the Magnificat *"Regale"* are early works, composed before 1502, since all three titles are listed in the original index of the Eton Choirbook (Windsor, Eton College, MS 178).[11] An entry in the records of King's College, Cambridge, of 1503–4 shows that Jaxson, a chaplain, received eight shillings for copying two masses (both anonymous), one of which is called *Regali ex progenie.* Since no mass with this title other than that by Fayrfax is known from the sources, it is believed that Fayrfax was the composer of the Mass *Regali ex progenie* copied by Jaxson. This would place the date of the Fayrfax mass no later than 1503–4. Another entry, this one in the records of King's College, Cambridge, for 1508–9, shows that John Sygar, a composer and chaplain, was paid for copying seven sequences from the compositions of Fayrfax and Cornysh (d. 1523) and three sequences for Advent. The lost sequences mentioned above are believed to be among those copied by Sygar.[12]

Two antiphons composed in homage to members of the royal household can be dated. *Lauda vivi Alpha et O*, a litany of praise to the Blessed Virgin Mary, concludes with a prayer for Henry VIII, beginning "O rosa gratiae," and therefore would have been composed at the earliest in 1509, the year of the king's coronation.

It has been generally assumed that the following entry in 1502 in the Privy Purse Expense Book of Queen Elizabeth of York refers to the antiphon *Aeterne laudis lilium:*

> Thies ar the Payments made the xxiiijte: Day of Marche, Anno xvij mo . . . to Robert Fayrfax for setting an Antheme of oure Lady and Saint Elizabeth, in rewarde, XX, s.[13]

The queen visited St. Albans in 1502, and it is believed that the antiphon may have been composed for that event. Not only does the year of her visit coincide with that of the record of payment, but in the musical setting, reference in the text to Saint Elizabeth shows repetition and elaboration of Elizabeth's name (mm. 132–37). Repetition of words in Fayrfax's music is unusual. Previously unnoticed but equally significant for understanding the intent of Fayrfax's setting is the fact that the poem in its original medieval Latin is an acrostic reading "Elisabeth regina anglie."

E	eterne laudis lilium o dulcis maria
L	laudat te vox angelica nutrix cristi pia
I	iure prolis glorie datur armonia
S	salus nostre memorie omni agonia
A	ave radix flos virginum o sanctificata
B	benedicta in utero materno creata
E	eras sancta puerpera et inviolata
T	tuo ex jhesu filio virgo peramata
H	honestis celi precibus virgo veneraris
R	regis excelsi filii visu iocundaris
E	eius divino lumine tu nusquam privaris
G	gaude sole splendidior virgo singularis
I	isakar quoque nazaphat necnon ismaria
N	natus ex jesse stipite qua venit maria
A	atque maria cleophe sancto zacharia
A	a quo patre ELISABETH matre sophonia
N	natus est dei gracia johannes baptista
G	gaudebat clauso domino in matrice cista
L	linee ex hoc genere est evangelista
I	johannes anne filia ex maria ista
E	est jhesu dei filium natus in hunc mundum
	cuius cruoris tumulo mundatur immundum
	conferat nos in gaudium in evum iocundum
	qui cum patre et spiritu sancto regnat in unum
	amen[14]

The renown of Fayrfax continued long after his death. Thomas Morley includes Fayrfax in the list of Englishmen whose music he has drawn upon for his *Plaine and Easie Introduction to Practicall Musicke (1597).*[15] And Anthony à Wood (d. 1695) wrote in the seventeenth century that he had seen some of his music and that Fayrfax was "in great renowne and counted Prime Musitian of the Nation."[16]

The Principal Forms of Sacred Polyphony

Throughout the late fifteenth century and until the Reformation the principal forms of sacred polyphony in England were the mass, the Magnificat, and the votive antiphon. They were large works written for important religious festivals. They also reflect the particular fervor with which the cult of the Virgin was practiced in England and the special role which music occupied in the Marian rites.

The five or six voices for which they were composed cover a total range of about three octaves, providing the opportunity for massive choral sonority and a wide spectrum of vocal color. Sections of counterpoint for the complete number of voices (with a plainsong placed as cantus firmus in the tenor) contrast with freely composed sections for two and three parts. These sections were disposed in such a way as to form a musical design for each work as a whole.[17]

In the settings of the mass and Magnificat there were traditions for placement of the full chorus and of those sections written for fewer parts. In the music of this edition these traditions may be seen in the use of the full five-part ensemble for "Gratias agimus" in the Gloria, whereas, for example, less than the full number of voices is called for in the "Benedictus qui venit" of the Sanctus and in the eighth verse in the Magnificat. But for the votive antiphon only those texts which were set frequently over a period of time show evidence of such conventions being applied (see the evocations and tropes in Fayrfax's *Salve regina*, for example). Within these traditions Tudor composers found considerable flexibility, relying upon a multiplicity of contrapuntal styles and techniques and upon the effect of juxtaposing the full sound of the complete chorus and the softer sound of counterpoint for a reduced number of parts.

Metrical changes from triple to duple time in the large votive antiphon and in single movements of the mass, and a return to triple meter in the Magnificat, establish bipartite or tripartite divisions of the form. It is only in the short votive antiphon for four voices that triple meter may be absent and duple meter employed throughout.

Magnificats and votive antiphons are known in sufficient number from the Eton Choirbook and other sources to provide an understanding of how these two forms developed in England after Dunstable. But relatively few masses have survived the great loss of manuscripts from this period. Fayrfax and his young contemporary Nicholas Ludford (died in or after 1557) are the only early Tudor composers whose masses are known to any degree.

The Mass

Early Tudor masses are cyclic works in which both a motto and a cantus firmus unify the work as a whole. They consist of four movements (not five as on the Continent) that are approximately equal in length. The Kyrie, which in England was troped at festivals, and thus was more a part of the Proper than the Ordinary, was traditionally omitted from polyphonic settings of the mass in England.[18] Shortening of the text of the Credo and of the Gloria by means of telescoping seems to have been favored by the English. This technique of setting different portions of the text simultaneously in different voice parts or of using double texts in a single voice part appears early in the fifteenth century.[19] Later, at the time of Fayrfax, English composers favored shortening the text of the Credo by excisions which vary in number and length. The reason for abbreviating the text is not documented, but it is thought to have been introduced as a way to make the Gloria and Credo equal in length.[20] Settings of the relatively short texts of the Sanctus and Agnus Dei, on the other hand, were extended by long passages of florid, melismatic counterpoint.

These masses were characteristically composed on a tenor cantus firmus drawn from a plainsong. A high proportion are Marian masses, so-called because the plainsong is from the Office of the Virgin. The cantus firmus is a structural part in sections set for the complete chorus, and it does not normally migrate from the tenor voice.

The motto consists of one, several, or all of the voices with which the first movement begins. This opening is then repeated, usually with some variants, for the beginning of all subsequent movements. The individual parts (or part) which constitute the motto may move without pause directly into the counterpoint that follows. In this case the motto serves as a springboard for the counterpoint that follows in each movement. But the most distinctive motto and the one perhaps heard most clearly is that of a short section closing with a cadence and fermata. (One sees this, for example, in the Mass *O bone Jesu* by Fayrfax.) Reference to the opening of the plainsong melody may be introduced as part of the motto, but use of the head of the plainsong melody at this point is independent of the function of the chant as the tenor cantus firmus throughout the movement in sections for the full chorus. In an individual movement of the mass, the first statement of the cantus firmus comes only with the entrance of the full chorus after one or more sections of free counterpoint in two or three parts.

The Magnificat

As Mary's response to her cousin Elizabeth's greeting recognizing her as the Mother of the Lord, the Magnificat was a significant part of the worship of the Blessed Virgin, occupying a central position at vespers. It consists of the ten verses from the Gospel (Luke 1: 46–55), similar in form to those of a psalm, and concludes with the Lesser Doxology, bringing the total number of verses to twelve.

English composers preferred polyphonic settings of the even-numbered verses sung *alternatim* with the chanting of the odd-numbered verses on one of the eight plainsong Tones. They were, therefore, works of six polyphonic movements. These were grouped into three pairs by changes of meter: the middle verses (six and eight), in duple time, were enclosed by verses two and four and verses ten and twelve, all in triple meter. The three-part form which is established by the changes in meter was unified by the use of a cantus firmus.

The cantus firmus was a faburden to the Magnificat Tone with which the polyphonically set verses alternated, unlike the Continental settings in which the Magnificat Tone itself served as cantus firmus.[21] In the Magnificat, the cantus firmus was treated more freely than in the mass; the opening and termination of the faburden were clearly stated, but otherwise the borrowed material was disguised by ornamentation or abandoned altogether.

The polyphonic verses were composed so as to provide contrast as the performance of the work progressed. At the same time, the sequence of musical events and references in the text establishes a large overall musical design. This is true of all the principal forms of sacred polyphony, but it is particularly evident in the settings of the Magnificat. The English composer seems to have been sensitive to the restrictions of the simple verse form of the Magnificat and aware of the benefits to be gained by superimposing a musical form upon that of the given text.

As stated above, the English composer followed certain traditions in setting the Magnificat. According to Doe, the full five- (or six-) part chorus was employed for verses two and six, for "Abraham" in verse ten, and for the second half or for only the conclusion of verses ten and twelve. Counterpoint for less than the complete number of parts, usually two or three parts, was reserved for verses four and eight and for portions of verses ten and twelve.[22] The full chorus, therefore, was usually placed at the opening and close of the Magnificat and at the beginning of the pair of verses in duple meter. The most florid counterpoint was reserved for verse eight, set for less than the full number of parts.

The Votive Antiphon

One of the most interesting aspects of religious

practice and the Marian cult in England was the singing of votive antiphons in monastic cathedrals and secular abbeys, in chapels of the royal court and great households, and in colleges and universities.[23] The large repertory in the Eton Choirbook alone demonstrates the extent to which this sacred form occupied the English composer.[24]

In contrast to the prose of the mass or the psalm-like verses of the Magnificat, the texts of the votive antiphon were rhymed poetry, ordinarily of great length. They were originally drawn from the Processional, Antiphonary, or Sequentiary, but in later development, non-ritual texts from Books of Hours and other devotional books were added.

The large votive antiphon for five or more voices was a long work, on the average shorter than a Magnificat but longer than a movement of a festal mass, which it resembled in design. Many were written with a free tenor, but perhaps more often they were composed on a cantus firmus taken from a plainsong unrelated to the antiphon text. In the Eton Choirbook approximately a third of the antiphons composed on a cantus firmus open in a manner similar to the motto of a mass, with reference to the plainsong.

When a mass and votive antiphon were linked, the cantus firmus or motto (or both) were used to bring about this relationship. Two antiphons by Fayrfax, *O Maria deo grata* and *Gaude flore virginali*, may, for example, have been composed with this intent. In Tenbury MS 1464 (a single bass part) the antiphon *O Maria deo grata* is inscribed "O Maria deo grata or Albanus" (fols. 17v and 20r), while *Gaude flore virginali* reads "Gaude flore or regali" (fol. 22r) and at its conclusion "Finis regali" (fol. 24r). In the first instance the presence of the motive from the "Albanus" plainsong, used at the beginning and conclusion of the antiphon in contrapuntal procedures like those found in the Mass *Albanus*, seems to indicate that the antiphon and mass are linked. The tenor for the antiphon, however, has not survived. The real relation of *Gaude flore virginali* to the Mass *Regali*, however, cannot be determined, since only the bassus of the antiphon is known, and it shows no musical relationship to the bassus of the mass.

A third antiphon, *O bone Jesu*, assumed to be by Fayrfax, of which only the medius part is known (Harley MS 1708, fols. 53v–55r), shows that it served as the model for his Mass *O bone Jesu*. Fayrfax's Magnificat *O bone Jesu* is also musically related to these two works.[25]

Reflecting a perhaps less common compositional technique, the four complete votive antiphons for five voices by Fayrfax (*Salve regina, Aeterne laudis lilium, Ave Dei patris filia,* and *Maria plena virtute*) are freely composed. The setting of the *Salve regina*, included in the Eton Choirbook and therefore an early work, is in a florid style not found in his other works—but a style which is nevertheless conservative in relation to such works in the Eton Choirbook as the settings of *Salve re-*

gina by Richard Davy and William Cornysh or John Browne's *O regina mundi clara*.[26] *Ave Dei patris filia* was the most widely known of all Fayrfax's works. Although apparently otherwise written on a freely composed tenor, the antiphon nevertheless opens with a quotation and contrapuntal development of the first two melodic phrases of the *Salve regina* plainsong. In the three-part counterpoint with which the antiphon begins, the superius and contratenor share in presenting and elaborating upon the plainsong (mm. 1–9). The medius is an independent part. *Maria plena virtute*, by the very nature of its Passion text, is composed in a sustained, deliberate manner in which florid, melismatic melodic movement and complex rhythms are absent. The flexibility of the scoring, exposed imitation, strong cadences, and darkening of the mode by the use of three flats place this work in contrast to the other three antiphons. In relation to the *Salve regina*, for instance, it shows that a change took place in the course of Fayrfax's musical life.

The Music of This Edition

Mass Regali ex progenie

Of all Fayrfax's masses the Mass *Regali ex progenie* is considered most representative of conventional practice at the turn of the fifteenth century.[27] It is a cyclic work in the customary four movements, composed on a tenor cantus firmus serving as the structural voice in contrapuntal sections for the full chorus and with a motto at the opening of each movement. Since the plainsong for the cantus firmus is taken from the Office of the Virgin, it is a Marian mass.

This mass is one of four festal masses for five voices (the Mass *O bone Jesu* is a votive mass) and one of three composed for a chorus in a normal range. The Mass *Albanus*, like the antiphon *Aeterne laudis lilium*, is for high voices; the Mass *O bone Jesu* is for a low chorus.

The five voices cover an overall span of three octaves from low F in the bassus to f″ in the highest voice. The two high voices exactly duplicate the ranges of the contratenor and bassus at an octave above, while the tenor sings in the same range as the contratenor. This is important to note for an understanding of the rich, sometimes heavy sound in the low range of the counterpoint for the complete number of parts and for the crossing of voices, particularly when both the contratenor and tenor are involved in three- or four-part writing.

The first five measures with which the Gloria opens are repeated with minor variants in subsequent movements as the motto for the mass. This motto, in four-voice, non-imitative counterpoint, is freely composed; there is no reference to the plainsong on which the mass is composed (see Example 1).

Example 1.
Plainsong *Regali ex progenie*, transcribed by the present editor from the facsimile in the *Antiphonale sarisburiense*, ed. Walter H. Frere (London, 1901–24), pl. 526.

The plainsong melody of the cantus firmus is stated twice in the Gloria, three times in the Credo, once in the Sanctus, and once in the Agnus Dei. Except for the Credo, the cantus firmus is presented only in sections for the full chorus. In the Gloria, Fayrfax first divides the melody of the chant at its mid-point (it is interrupted at the end of the second staff in the example), placing the first half of the chant in the "Gratias agimus" section (mm. 27–56) and the second half (starting with "nos" in the chant) in the "Domine Deus" section (mm. 72–88). The chant is then presented a second time, without interruption, for the full-chorus "Que sedes" section (mm. 128–69), with which the movement concludes. The Credo differs from the Gloria and the other two movements in that the cantus firmus is present in all sections but two: the section with which the Credo begins (mm. 1–29) and the "Et incarnatus" section (mm. 83–104), which opens the second half of the movement. Consequently the cantus firmus provides the basis for the counterpoint in sections for less than the full number of parts as well as in those for the full chorus. The first complete statement of the chant extends from m. 29 through the conclusion of the first half of the movement at m. 82. This includes the three-part "Genitum non factum" section (mm. 59–69, for superius, medius, and tenor) and the full-chorus "Et in unum" (mm. 29–58) and "Qui propter nos homines" sections (mm. 69–82), which precede and follow it. In relation to the disposition of the chant melody, it should be noted that the mid-point of the chant (after "precibus") is reached at the conclusion of the "Et in unum" section, matching in length the twenty-nine measures of counterpoint of the "Gratias agimus" section in the Gloria. It is interesting, for it is reminiscent of isorhythmic procedures. In each of its two subsequent statements in the Credo, the chant is also complete. The cantus firmus is placed in the tenor for the setting of the Crucifixus for contratenor, tenor, and bassus (mm. 104–25), and its final note serves as the first note of the concluding section of the movement, the full-chorus "Et resurrexit" (mm. 125–66). The Sanctus and Agnus Dei are conceived as a pair in relation to the scoring for the two opening sections in each movement as well as in the disposition of the cantus firmus and the melody of the borrowed chant. The scheme is the same for both movements. The plainsong is broken into three fragments (23 + 14 + 20 notes, respectively), each of which serves as cantus firmus for the three full-choral sections in each movement. This use of the cantus firmus is more traditional than that for the Credo or even for the Gloria. It is also reminiscent of procedures employed earlier in the century when individual movements of the Ordinary were paired: the Gloria and the Credo, the Sanctus and Agnus Dei. It is important to observe that the rhythmic design and length (in terms of measures in the score) of the cantus firmus statements in the Sanctus are not repeated in the Agnus Dei.

Throughout the mass, the chant is presented for the most part without embellishment; interpolations occur at the final cadences in the Gloria and Agnus Dei; pitches may be lengthened by repetition or elongation, but melodically the chant is unaltered. It moves in notes slightly longer than those of the contrapuntal voices that surround it, and it is generally detached from their melodic or rhythmic figurations. A notable exception occurs in the Crucifixus of the Credo (mm. 104–25), where, although the melody of the chant is not changed, it is briefly caught up in the rhythmic movement of the outer voices during the long melisma and drive to the cadence (mm. 115–23).

The cantus firmus remains in the tenor throughout, with two exceptions. In the opening of the Crucifixus for contratenor, tenor, and bassus, the head of the chant is heard briefly in the contratenor before being taken up by the tenor moving in long notes (Credo, mm. 104–6). The tenor is singing above the contratenor at this point so that the placement of the cantus firmus in the contratenor is disguised. And at the close of the mass, in the setting of "pacem" (Agnus Dei, mm. 136–41), the contratenor introduces the concluding section of the cantus firmus in a series of imitative entrances that move from the contratenor, to the tenor, and finally to the bassus. Such an event is characteristic of Fayrfax's treatment of the conclusion of the mass as a point of special musical interest—a rounding-off, a climax to the work as a whole (see his Mass *Albanus* and Mass *Tecum principium*).

Magnificat "Regale"

The significance of the title *"Regale"* for this Magnificat remains unknown. In the Lambeth Choirbook the word *"Regale"* is inscribed above the superius at the first opening (fol. 67v), in the place normally used for the name of the composer, and again on the staff of the bassus following the conclusion of this part. There is no apparent musical relationship to the Mass *Regali ex progenie* nor to the bassus of the antiphon *Gaude flore virginali* (see discussion above). Hughes's suggestion that it refers to King's College, Cambridge—a *collegium regale*—and for which it may have been intended, has been generally accepted.[28]

In this Magnificat, the even-numbered verses in counterpoint are intended to alternate with the chanting of Tone VIII transposed down a fifth. (The transposed chant has been editorially supplied in the edition.) The faburden to this Tone is used as the cantus firmus (see Example 2 and note 21).

Example 2.
Faburden to Magnificat Tone VIII with second ending, transcribed by Paul Doe, *Early Tudor Magnificats: I* (London, 1962): 137.

Et ex- sul- ta- vit ___ spi- ri- tus me-

- - us in De- -

- o sa- lu- ta- ri me- o.

The movement up a fourth, with which both the Tone and faburden begin, functions in various forms as a motto in all verses. The opening of the faburden and its termination are quoted faithfully, especially the termination ("salutari meo," mm. 12–15 of the faburden), which is presented deliberately and with clarity. But after the opening measures the faburden melody is obscured; the tenor may become virtually free.

Typical of its treatment in all three sacred forms, the cantus firmus is associated with sections for the full chorus. Curiously, in this Magnificat Fayrfax uses the chorus in only three verses: the second, set throughout for the five-voice chorus (mm. 1–28); the sixth, in which the chorus opens and closes the verse (mm. 72–83 and mm. 102–8, respectively); and the concluding section of the Magnificat (mm. 228–36), a setting of the final word of the text "saeculorum" followed by the "Amen."

Although the verses are linked by motto or cantus firmus, by mode, and by recurrent cadencing to the Final, each of the six verses is unique, resulting in a series of six strongly contrasting movements. In the scoring for counterpoint for less than the full chorus, Fayrfax repeats a particular combination of voices only once: the scoring of contratenor, tenor, and bassus for the melismatic setting of the word "dispersit" (mm. 83–90) at the beginning of the second half of the sixth verse reappears for the tenth verse (mm. 143–93). The latter, which refers to the fulfillment of the Prophecy, is composed throughout for the three low voices.

The eighth verse (mm. 109–42) is interesting for its counterpoint in four parts and for its melismatic passages in a florid and rhythmically complex style. In addition, the presence of the cantus firmus points to this verse as significant in the design of the work as a whole, since it introduces the third statement of the cantus firmus.

The tenth verse is also of particular interest for the high concentration of imitation in all three voices (mm. 154–59, 169–71, and 176–78), as well as for the contratenor and tenor in duet, moving in the same range and constantly crossing the bassus. Imitation is not syntactically used but appears throughout the verse at the beginning of phrases and in the long melismas. And Fayrfax relates the beginning of the second half of this verse to that of its first half, as well as to the opening of the Magnificat, by repeating a melodic and rhythmic idea characterized by two sixteenths. It should also be noted that the setting of "Abraham" (mm. 169–75) is for three voice parts, rather than for the customary full chorus. It is possible that the carefully spaced entrances of the voices in strict imitation were considered a form of word emphasis.

Aeterne laudis lilium

Aeterne laudis lilium is a large votive antiphon for five voices in a high composite range (the equivalent of two sopranos, two high tenors, and baritone), extending twenty-one notes from the B-flat in the bassus to the high a" of the superius. There is no cantus firmus; all five voices are freely composed. The voices are alike in rhythm and melodic movement. They consequently share equally in the development of the counterpoint.

The words of *Aeterne laudis lilium* are those of a nonritual text, and, in view of the acrostic, they were undoubtedly written specifically to honor the queen. The text is a poem that consists of six four-line verses. The first three, in praise of the Blessed Virgin Mary, follow a rhyme scheme in which the lines of the first two verses repeatedly close on the vowel "a," the lines of the third verse on the sibilant "is." The second three verses recount the genealogy of Christ, in which reference is made to the Visitation and Saint Elizabeth. These three verses follow a pattern similar to that of the first three: the lines of the first two verses (verses 4 and 5) close on "a," those of the third (verse 6) on "um." The poem thus divides into two parts—a bipartite division of the six verses that is followed by Fayrfax in his musical setting.

This antiphon is a classic example of the English composer's interest in the design and proportion of a work as a whole and of the skill with which these concepts were realized by Fayrfax. The bipartite musical setting is symmetrical; the six four-line verses of the poem are distributed so that three correspond to each half of the antiphon. The first three verses (mm. 1–104), in praise of the Blessed Virgin Mary, are composed as three sections, approximately equal in length, and in triple meter. The first two are for less than the five parts (a section for superius, medius, and contratenor, mm. 1–38, followed by one for contratenor, tenor, and bassus, mm. 38–71). The third section (mm. 71–104), which closes the first half of the antiphon, is for the full sonority of the five parts. Melismas on the penultimate syllables of the final line of each verse direct attention to the strophic form of the text and provide relief from the strictly syllabic style that otherwise prevails.

In the second half (mm. 105–213), in duple meter, Fayrfax disregards the four-line verse form of the poem and divides the recounting of the genealogy of Christ into two six-line segments. Consequently, in contrast to the first half of the antiphon, the second half is composed of two sections. The first (mm. 105–57) is scored for two- or three-part counterpoint, a series of contrasting sections of counterpoint that change as to range and voice color. The second (mm. 157–213), with which the antiphon closes, is for the full five-part chorus.

It is in the first part (mm. 105–57), scored for two or three voice parts, that the Visitation of Mary is mentioned and reference is made to Elizabeth. In his setting, Fayrfax places the reference to Elizabeth and homage to the queen at the center of these fifty-two measures. References to Mary (mm. 105–26) and, later, to John the Baptist rejoicing in his mother's womb (mm. 140–57) precede and follow the homage. The words "Maria" and "cista" (womb) are given special emphasis by means of melismas (mm. 117–26 and 149–57, respectively) that are unusually long for the customary syllabic settings of antiphon texts and may point to the royal occasion for which the antiphon was written. The deliberately spaced entrances by each of the five parts with the queen's name (mm. 132–37), sung to a four-note motive reminiscent of the opening of the antiphon, are planned so as to form a musical arch. The entrance of the superius rising to a high a", a thirteenth above the contratenor, is the keystone. It is important to observe that, although all five voice parts are involved in the homage, they are never heard at the same time; there are no more than three in counterpoint at any given moment. Two facts are interesting: first, that Fayrfax chose the lighter sound of less than the full sonority of five parts for the homage, and second, that in doing so he was careful to retain that effect at the moment when all five parts were involved in im-

itative counterpoint singing the queen's name. The full sonority of five-part counterpoint is delayed, as it were, until the statement in the text that begins "Lineae ex hoc genere." Is this an oblique reference to the lineage of the houses of York and Tudor and heirs to the throne?

The genealogy of Christ, which continues with references to his birth and sacrifice and the joy conferred upon mankind, is completed in the choral section. The setting is syllabic, the counterpoint almost entirely consonant and sustained; the parts move by thirds and fourths in an essentially non-melodic fashion until the "Amen," where the antiphon is brought to a brilliant conclusion with leaping fifths and rising scalar motion in imitation in all voices. And the superius line holds the third of the final harmony, a high a".

In the Lambeth Choirbook the name of the contratenor part is inscribed in the left-hand margin at the beginning of the antiphon (fol. 56v). It stands next to the ornamental letter for this voice and just below the marginal decoration (see Plate I). It is the only voice named in the manuscript. If there is any significance for singling out this voice, it may be that the contratenor sings all but one-and-one-half lines of the entire poem ("Atque Maria Cleophae, sancto Zacharia, A quo patre" is omitted). This voice, then, is heard throughout the antiphon, dropping out only for seven measures (mm. 126–32) to re-enter with the name "Elizabeth" (m. 133). Also to be noticed is that in this section the medius sings only the four-note motive for "Elizabeth" (mm. 136–37), nothing more, with interesting visual results in the manuscript (fol. 58v). "Elizabeth" and the four notes, preceded and followed by a long series of rests, are inscribed as the only musical event on the single staff drawn across the bottom of the folio.

The Musical Style

The counterpoint in these three works by Fayrfax is distinguished by florid melodic movement, by complex rhythm, and by the resonance of imperfect consonance and minimal use of dissonance. In its ornamental style, complexity of rhythm, and retention of triple meter, it is an extension of earlier musical attitudes. In its consonance, it is peculiarly English.

It is primarily in counterpoint for five or more voices that one finds a predominantly harmonic or chordal effect and almost completely unrelieved consonance. When composed on a cantus firmus, the movement of individual voices is restricted by the sustaining of the cantus firmus by the tenor, but even when the tenor is freely composed, as in *Aeterne laudis lilium*, the harmonic changes are deliberate and the voices progress essentially from one "chord" tone to the next. Imitation is not excluded, nor is a certain freedom of melodic movement, but there is a tendency toward circular, sometimes awkward lines governed by thirds and fourths (see e.g., Gloria, mm. 128–39 and 153–61; *Aeterne*, mm. 177–83).

While the writing for five voices relies upon harmonic and choral effects, counterpoint for two or three voice parts is composed with an attention to detail and in a style that demands great skill from the composer and the singers. In duets the voices function equally in the counterpoint. When three voices are involved, the relationships may vary from three equal parts widely spaced or crossing, to two in duet over a supporting voice, to one part moving independently over the other two. These relationships are established at the outset of a section and remain fairly constant throughout (e.g., Gloria, mm. 14–27; Agnus Dei, mm. 19–35; Sanctus, mm. 58–72).

In general much of this music is non-imitative. Nevertheless, imitation is characteristic of counterpoint for less than five parts. It serves to introduce voices at the beginning of a section (e.g., Magnificat, mm. 29–32) and to introduce or accentuate single words or phrases of text (e.g., *Aeterne*, mm. 41–44). Or imitation may emerge in the course of a long, florid passage, embellishing and giving shape to the counterpoint. Used in conjunction with repeated or sequenced motives or phrases, it accelerates the movement toward a cadence (e.g., *Aeterne*, mm. 30–38; Magnificat, mm. 66–71; Gloria, mm. 96–112; Sanctus, mm. 116–37).

Unusually long, non-cadencing contrapuntal passages in a melismatic, ornamental style are one of the most interesting aspects of the music of Fayrfax and his contemporaries. In settings of one or two words the precise placement of the syllables suggests that vocalizing the particular sound of the vowel and the process of changing it in different voices at different times are important in directing the counterpoint and giving it shades of color. When the passage is very long, as in the Benedictus (i.e., Sanctus, mm. 111–50), the meaning of the text may give way to the brilliance of the singing and to the pure expression of religious fervor. The vocal style required to control unexpected endings of melodic phrases followed quickly by reentrance or the inflection in moving from a short note to one of longer duration on a syllable or new phrase (e.g., Sanctus, mm. 118–20) further intensifies the improvisatory style. Is it this jubilating that aroused the scorn of the Continental composers?

The counterpoint relies on a pervasive use of syncopation and off-beat accents, hemiola, irregular groupings within the measure, and the bridging of the barline in the modern score (e.g., Gloria, mm. 107–12; Agnus Dei, mm. 83–94; Magnificat, mm. 46–52). These devices play perhaps a more important role than dissonance in generating the flow of the contrapuntal voices.

Dissonance conforms to the practice of the time; anomalous dissonances are rare. Passing notes, suspensions, and anticipations are used most frequently, as well as the upper turning note (later, with the recognition of triads, labeled an *échappée*). Cambiatas and neighboring tones appear less often. The appoggiatura, prepared and unprepared, is used by Fayrfax with particular effectiveness (see the close of his Mass *Tecum principium* for a series of unprepared appoggiaturas moving through the five voices). The expressiveness of a sixth (an imperfect consonance) resolving to a fifth is also recognized by Fayrfax (see e.g., Gloria, mm. 5–6, where a six-three "chord" moves to a five-three). And in the cadence the sixth may be heard as a suspension, appoggiatura, or upper neighboring tone, delaying the resolution of all voices until the final harmony (e.g., Magnificat, mm. 70–71 and 215–18).

The variety of cadences and the absence of a standardized use of suspension formulae are characteristic of the late fifteenth century and point to the period as one of transition. The bassus may prepare for the cadence in movement by leaps of fourths or fifths, leading directly from the fifth or fourth degree of the mode to its Final (V–I cadences are favored). English preference for the sound of the third may be heard in the complete triad in the final harmony in all five-voice cadences and in the use of the octave with the third rather than with the fifth in three-part counterpoint.

The most curious cadence in the three works may be heard in the Agnus Dei (mm. 90–94), where, after strong harmonic movement in the bassus, the harmony resolves deceptively up a third, from G to B-flat. The superius descends by scalar motion from e" to e', then ascends to e" and turns in the manner of an upper neighboring tone (and therefore editorially inflected by a flat in the score) to resolve on d", doubling the third in the final B-flat harmony.

The traditional use of the third in English music may be noted not only in the third and occasional double-third at the cadence but also in sections in nonquartal counterpoint (e.g., Gloria, mm. 112–27; Magnificat, mm. 53–71) and in the frequency with which two voices cross, at times in the style of gymel (e.g., Agnus Dei, mm. 26–35). This sound, the resonance of the imperfect consonance that permeates the music of Fayrfax and indeed that of his English contemporaries, has its origin in faburden.

Suggestions for Performance

The tempo should be moderate (66 to 72 quarternotes per minute), slow enough to accommodate easily the shorter note values but not so slow as to prevent a lively interplay of the rhythmic patterns and cross accenting among the voices.

To prevent blurring of the rhythmic patterns, which should remain exact, clearly articulated, and free of any metrical stress implied by the modern use of the barline, a chorus of about twenty voices using a straight tone is recommended. It is probable that sections in the Magnificat and *Aeterne laudis lilium* in which the source text is inscribed in red ink (italicized text in the edition) were sung by a single voice on a part (see below under Lambeth Palace, MS 1 and note 36). It is recommended that these sections be sung by a single voice to a part or by a half chorus.

The intonations "Gloria in excelsis Deo," for the Gloria, and "Credo in unum Deo," for the Credo, were chanted by the priest and therefore were not included in polyphonic settings. The intonation for Gloria V (*Liber usualis* [Desclee: Tournai, 1961], 28) or Gloria III (*Liber usualis*, p. 23) is recommended for the performance of the Gloria; Credo I (*Liber usualis*, p. 64) is recommended for the Credo. The chant intonations should be transposed down a fifth, as shown in Example 3, or up a fourth, and each should be sung by a solo voice.[29] According to Warren, the Magnificat plainsong Tone (editorially supplied in the edition for the chanting of the odd-numbered verses) should be sung by a solo voice.[30] Performance by a half chorus is also recommended.

Example 3.

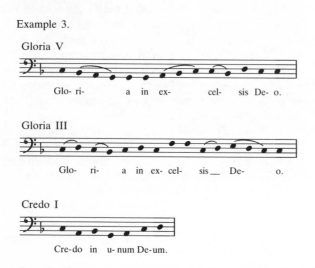

Gloria V

Glo- ri- a in ex- cel- sis De- o.

Gloria III

Glo- ri- a in ex- cel- sis__ De- o.

Credo I

Cre-do in u- num De-um.

Instruments may be used to double voice parts or to substitute for them.[31] Instrumental doubling for the tenor cantus firmus in the five-voice sections of the mass, for instance, would be effective. *Aeterne laudis lilium*, which is composed in a high range, may be transposed down a fourth.[32]

Lambeth Palace, MS 1

Today three giant choirbooks provide the principal sources for sacred music in England between the time of Dunstable and that of Taverner (ca. 1453–1545): Eton College, MS 178, at Windsor; Lambeth Palace, MS 1, in London; and the Gonville and Caius College, MS 667, at Cambridge.

The Lambeth Choirbook, measuring 67 x 46.8 cm.,

has survived intact and in a fine state of preservation. Hughes considered it a primary source for the sacred music of Fayrfax; it is the most reliable as to date and contents, and its pages are often marked as having been corrected.[33]

Edward Higgons is believed to have copied the Lambeth Choirbook during the 1520s for use at St. Stephen's, Westminster.[34] (Higgons was a canon at St. Stephen's in 1518.) The illuminations and lack of economy in the use of parchment, in fact, indicate that it was destined for a chapel of high rank and wealth, while the Tudor rose in marginal decorations as well as the H and 8, superimposed on the decorated initial at the opening of the Mass *Regali ex progenie* (fol. 79v), point specifically to the royal court and the reign of Henry VIII.

The music of the choirbook is written in full black notation with white (black void) for imperfection and for the semiminima and fusa. There are exceptions. The antiphon *Aeterne laudis lilium* (see Plates I and II), the Magnificat *O bone Jesu*, and the Magnificat "*Regale*," by Fayrfax, as well as the Mass *Benedicta*, by Ludford, are notated in full black notes with full red notes for imperfection and for the semiminima and fusa. Notation in white notes with black notes for imperfection and for the semiminima and fusa appears only for the anonymous antiphon *Gaude flore virginali*, which stands approximately at the center of the manuscript.

Of particular interest is the scribe's use of red ink for portions of the text. Black ink is used for almost all works, but the use of red ink for portions of the text set for less than the full number of parts may be seen in the three works by Fayrfax mentioned above and also in Stourton's *Ave Maria ancilla trinitatis*.[35] The practice of coloring portions of the text in English manuscripts reaches back into the beginnings of choral polyphony early in the fifteenth century and continues until the end of the century. Its appearance in the Lambeth Choirbook is a late example of this practice. Andrew Hughes finds that red ink was employed to signal solo as opposed to choral performance and that it was always associated with portions of the text set for a reduced number of parts.[36]

There are nineteen compositions in the Lambeth Choirbook: seven masses, four Magnificats, and eight antiphons. Four masses are placed at the beginning, three at the close. Antiphons and Magnificats fill the space between.

The majority of the works are for five voices; only three are for six, and compositions for four voices are absent altogether. The composer's name is given for four of the nineteen works in the choirbook. The name "Stourton" is inscribed as the composer of the antiphon *Ave Maria ancilla trinitatis*. At the head of the second mass in the manuscript, an anonymous scribble in a later hand reads "O quam glorifica Doctor ffayrfax for his forme in proceadinge to bee doctor." The name "ffeyrfax" stands at the head of the antiphon *Aeterne laudis lilium* (see Plate 1); "fferfax" is inscribed for the Magnificat *O bone Jesu*. (Inconsistency in the spelling of a name was common at the time.) From other sources, primarily from the Caius Choirbook, it has been possible to identify composers for eight of the fifteen anonymous works: Fayrfax as the composer of four masses and of the Magnificat *"Regale,"* Ludford as the composer of two masses, and Lambe for the antiphon *O Maria plena gratia*.[37] Two Magnificats and five antiphons remain anonymous.

Thus the Lambeth Choirbook contains all the masses known to have been written by Fayrfax (except the incomplete Mass *Sponsus amat sponsam* for four voices), both extant Magnificats, and the antiphon *Aeterne laudis lilium*. It is the only choirbook of the three mentioned above that includes all three forms of sacred music. (The Eton Choirbook contains only antiphons and Magnificats; the Caius Choirbook only masses and Magnificats.)

The Edition

At the beginning of each work the original clef, flat signature, metrical sign, and initial note precede each voice. The range of each voice is shown in black stemless notes. Changes in metrical signs that occur in the manuscript in the course of a composition are indicated in the Critical Commentary. Ligatures are marked by closed brackets placed above the notes. Broken brackets indicate the use of full red or white notes for imperfection; the source's use of red or white notes for the semiminima and fusa is not specially marked in the edition. Editorially supplied additions are enclosed in square brackets.

Names of voice parts are not provided in the Lambeth Choirbook except for identification of the contratenor in the antiphon *Aeterne laudis lilium*. The terminology "medius," "contratenor," "tenor," and "bassus," given in works for five voices in the Eton Choirbook, has been adopted in the present edition. Since in Eton the highest voice is not named in works for five voices, this part has been editorially designated "superius."

The medieval Latin texts are given in modern church Latin, with punctuation and capitals as in present-day usage. In the Magnificat and antiphon, textual passages that are inscribed in red in the manuscript are indicated by italics. (For implications of this for performance, see Lambeth Palace, MS 1 above and note 36.) When a portion of the text is missing from the Lambeth Choirbook, and the reading is supplied from another source, this is shown by angle brackets and recorded in the Critical Commentary. When the underlaying of the missing text is supplied by the editor, it is enclosed in square brackets. In this edition the Magnificat Tone VIII for the odd-numbered verses has been

supplied by the editor from the Sarum Tonale[38] in conformity with the English traditional practice at this time.

The semibreve is transcribed as a quarter-note, a reduction to one-fourth its original value. This brings the transcription into conformity with present-day use of the quarter-note as the basic unit for a beat. Notes of shorter duration are beamed to show the frequent and characteristic shifting from 2 + 2 + 2 to 3 + 3 patterns in triple time and the irregular groupings, such as 3 + 3 + 2, in duple time. In order to suggest the flow of the line inherent in the original notation and to achieve clarity within the measure, ties are used only across the barline.

Editorial procedures for beaming eighth- and sixteenth-notes into groups are essentially those defined by Harrison in the preface to his edition of the Eton Choirbook.[39] For measures where the movement is by eighth-notes and in which no more than three successive sixteenths occur, notes are beamed in two- or four-note patterns, as in $\frac{3}{4}$ time, if the fourth eighth is not attacked (e.g., the third eighth may be dotted and followed by a sixteenth ♫ ♫. ♫). Notes are beamed in three-note patterns as in $\frac{6}{8}$ time if the third eighth is not attacked (e.g., the second eighth may be dotted and followed by a sixteenth ♫♫. ♫♫♫) and/ or if the fifth eighth is not attacked (e.g., the fourth eighth is dotted and is followed by a sixteenth ♫♫♫ ♫.♫♫). Measures containing a succession of eighth-notes, with no more than two successive sixteenth-notes, are beamed through the measure. The shape of a melodic line, the placement of a syllable, and, in a few instances, the dissonance may justify exceptions.

Editorial changes in the time signature are introduced when a rhythmic extension leading to a cadence at the close of sections or movements makes this necessary (e.g., the Gloria, m. 111; and mm. 70, 127, and 141 of the Magnificat). These metrical changes, along with single barlines throughout, have been editorially supplied.

Double bars in the transcription represent a line drawn through the staff at the close of sections in the manuscript. The final note with fermata in a cadence is a longa in the manuscript, unless indicated to the contrary in the Critical Commentary. It is transcribed according to modern usage so as to fit into the context of the music within the measure.

The matter of accidentals in the Lambeth Choirbook, as well as in those from Eton and Gonville and Caius colleges, is a continuing problem, still debated by scholars.[40] The issue involves how long an accidental is in effect, whether or not it is a later addition to the manuscript, and to what extent and where performers may have applied musica ficta.

In the manuscript an accidental applies only to the particular pitch, not its octave. It is valid only for the staff in which it occurs. An accidental may remain operative for the remainder of the staff, but no consistent method for canceling it is apparent. Each accidental, therefore, must be evaluated to determine how long it is actually in effect. Such editorial decisions, which are recorded in the Critical Commentary, are based upon the behavior of the individual line and the way it functions within the counterpoint. Resulting cross-relations should not be edited out.

In this edition accidentals are given as they appear in the source except that sharps in the manuscript are rendered as naturals when their intention is to cancel flats, and a flat cancelling a sharp is rendered as a natural. All discrepancies between source and edition regarding the placement of accidentals are recorded in the Critical Commentary. In accord with present-day practice, an accidental is understood here to be in effect only for the measure in which it falls. Accidentals obviously superfluous by modern convention have been removed and are recorded in the Critical Commentary. The position of accidentals in the manuscript that do not immediately precede the note affected is also recorded in the Critical Commentary. In the edition, accidentals on the staff are those notated in the manuscript, but a bracketed accidental on the staff indicates that, in the opinion of the editor, an accidental found earlier on the staff in the manuscript is still in effect. Accidentals above the staff are suggestions for performance according to our knowledge of the practice of musica ficta.

Critical Commentary

The primary source used as the basis of the present edition was the Lambeth Choirbook, London, Lambeth Palace, MS 1. The following commentary describes that source where it is at odds with the present edition. All references are to Lambeth unless otherwise noted. A list of concordant manuscript sources and modern editions is provided for each piece, but no attempt has been made to collate all variants in the text or music in these sources. The commentaries for the mass and the Magnificat also identify the cantus firmus and cite their respective sources.

In references to pitch notation, c' is used for middle C, c" for the octave above, and so forth. The voice-name designations are cited as S (= superius), Md (= medius), C (= contratenor), T (= tenor), and B (= bassus).

Mass Regali ex progenie

Sources: London, Lambeth Palace, MS 1 / Cambridge, Gonville and Caius College, MS 667 / Oxford, Bodleian Library, Arch F.e. 19–23 (formerly Mus. Sch. e 376–380) / Cambridge, University Library, MS Dd xiii.27 (contratenor) / Cambridge, St. John's College, MS 234 (bassus).

Modern edition: *Robert Fayrfax. Collected Works*, ed. Edwin B. Warren, 3 vols. (Rome, 1959–66), 1: 104–36.

Cantus firmus: *Regali ex progenie*, antiphon at Lauds on the Nativity of the Blessed Virgin Mary. Walter Frere, ed., *Antiphonale sarisburiense* (London, 1901–24), plate 526. In the *Liber usualis* (Tournai, 1938), 1626, it is the third antiphon for vespers on the Nativity of the Blessed Virgin Mary.[41]

GLORIA

Mm. 27–42, B, B-flat is omitted in signature. M. 27, Md, new staff begins with note 4; B-flat is omitted in the signature but is introduced for this staff preceding note 2, m. 28. M. 39, T, the setting of "tuam" has been omitted. M. 56, S, closes on a breve. Mm. 75–88, B, B-flat is omitted in signature. M. 76, Md, the rest is incorrectly notated as a minim-rest. M. 79, note 2–m. 88, T, B-flat is omitted in signature. M. 89, all voices, ¢. M. 92, C, note 3 is e in Bodleian.

CREDO

M. 1, all voices, ¢ . Mm. 35–37, T, "Jesum" underlies g and the ligature g–a, and "Christum" is under note 2, m. 37. Mm. 36–49, T, reading of text is from Bodleian. M. 43, note 4–m. 44, note 1, C, note is g, editorially emended from Bodleian. M. 74, T, "nos." Mm. 74–79, T, text is from Bodleian, its underlaying is editorial. M. 76, S, sharp for b' placed between notes 1 and 2. M. 80, Md, note 1 is b, editorially emended from Caius and Bodleian. M. 81, S, flat over note 2 cancels the sharp of m. 76. M. 83, all voices, ¢.

In order to show portions of the Credo omitted by Fayrfax in this mass, the complete text is given here with the missing portions printed in italics. The incipit "Credo in unum Deum," which is intoned by the priest and therefore not included in the contrapuntal setting, is enclosed in brackets.

[Credo in unum Deum,] Patrem omnipotentem, factorem caeli et terrae, visibilium omnium, et invisibilium. Et in unum Dominum Jesum Christum, Filium Dei unigenitum. Et ex Patre natum ante omnia saecula. *Deum de Deo, lumen de lumine, Deum verum de Deo vero.* Genitum, non factum, consubstantialem Patri: per quem omnia facta sunt. Qui propter nos homines, et propter nostram salutem descendit de caelis. Et incarnatus est de Spiritu Sancto ex Maria Virgine: Et homo factus est. Crucifixus etiam pro nobis: sub Pontio Pilato passus, et sepultus est. Et resurrexit tertia die, secundum Scripturas. Et ascendit in caelum: sedet ad dexteram Patris. *Et iterum venturus est cum gloria, judicare vivos et mortuos:* cujus regni non erit finis. *Et in Spiritum Sanctum, Dominum, et vivificantem: qui ex Patre Filioque procedit. Qui cum Patre et Filio simul adoratur, et conglorificatur: qui locutus est per Prophetas. Et unam sanctam catholicam et apostolicam Ecclesiam. Confiteor unum baptisma in remissionem peccatorum. Et expecto resurrectionem mortuorum.* Et vitam venturi saeculi. Amen.

Sanctus

M. 1, all voices, o . M. 45, C, flat canceling the sharp preceding note 1 placed over note 2. Mm. 51–53, B, text is from Caius. M. 92, C, note 3 is c, editorially emended according to all other sources. M. 111, Md, C, B,₵; S, T, ₵. M. 148, S, note 2 is d″ in Caius and Bodleian. M. 184, all voices, ♭ .

Agnus Dei

M. 1, all voices, ♭ . M. 69, B, the E-flat is not subsequently canceled on the staff which ends m. 80, note 2. M. 70, S closes on a breve. Mm. 73–78, T, reading of text is from Caius. M. 95, Md, ₵; all other voices, ₵. Mm. 128–30, C, text is "nobis," reading of "dona no-" is from Bodleian. "Regali" is inscribed below the staff of the B.

Magnificat "Regale"

Sources: London, Lambeth Palace, MS 1 / Cambridge, Gonville and Caius College, MS 667 / Cambridge, Peterhouse, MSS 471–74 (formerly MSS 40, 41, 31, 32) (tenor lacking) / Cambridge, University Library, MS Dd. xiii. 27 (contratenor) / Cambridge, St. John's College, MS 234 (bassus) / Fragments in British Museum, MS Add. 34191 and in Oxford, Bodleian Library, MS Lat. liturg. a 9 / Windsor, Eton College, MS 178 (the Magnificat is listed in the index, but the music has been lost from the manuscript).

Modern editions: *Robert Fayrfax. Collected Works*, ed. Edwin B. Warren, 3 vols. (Rome, 1959–66), 2:1–11. Frank Ll. Harrison, ed., *The Eton Choirbook: III*, Musica Britannica, vol. 12 (London, 1961), 96–103; *Robert Fayrfax. The Regali Magnificat*, The Fayrfax Series of Early English Choral Music, ed. Dom Anselm Hughes (London, 1949).

The plainsong Tone with which the polyphony alternates has been editorially added. It is the Magnificat Tone VIII with its second ending from the Sarum Tonale in *The Use of Sarum*, ed. Walter H. Frere (Cambridge, 1898–1901) ii, Appendix.

Cantus firmus: Faburden to Magnificat Tone VIII, in British Museum, MS Royal Appendix 56, fols. 23–25. Paul Doe, ed., *Early Tudor Magnificats: I*, vol. 4 of *Early English Church Music* (London, 1962), 137.

Throughout the Magnificat, cadences that mark the mid-point for each verse close on a breve with a fermata; cadences marking the conclusion of a verse are notated with a longa and fermata. Only the exceptions to this are recorded.

M. 28, Md, note is a breve. M. 52, T, note is a longa. M. 72, all voices, ₵. M. 123, B, an f above "bo" has been erased. M. 143, all voices, o . M. 168, B, note is a longa. M. 169, B, note 2, the e-flat of m. 164 is not canceled on the staff; a new staff line begins m. 169, note 4. M. 175, B, note is a longa. Mm. 180–81, B, starting m. 180, note 3, these two measures may be interpreted just as easily in $\frac{6}{8}$ time by articulating a descending sequential pattern of two sixteenths followed by two eighths. M. 216, C, note is a longa. M. 227, B, note is a longa.

Aeterne laudis lilium

Sources: London, Lambeth Palace, MS 1 / Edinburgh, National Library of Scotland, MS Adv. 5.1.15 (Scone Antiphonary) / Cambridge, Peterhouse, MSS 471–74 (formerly MSS 40, 41, 31, 32) (tenor lacking) / Cambridge, University Library, MS Dd. xiii.27 (contratenor) / Cambridge, St. John's College, MS 234 (bassus) / Tenbury, St. Michael's College, MS 1464 (bassus).

Modern edition: *Robert Fayrfax. Collected Works*, ed. Edwin B. Warren, 3 vols. (Rome, 1959–66), 2:47–56.

Mm. 9–11, S, Md, C, "Laudat te" in Scone and Cambridge University. M. 14, Md, "Christi" is not set. M. 23, S, sharp for note 4 placed below note 2. M. 24, S, "c," indicating cancellation of the sharp of m. 23, precedes note 1; M, "Salve." M. 28, C, note 3, new staff (which ends with m. 46, note 2); flat before e'. M. 29, S, flat for note 3 placed between notes 1 and 2. M. 31, S, sharp, canceling flat of m. 29 is placed below note 1 of this measure. M. 34, C, sharp canceling flat of m. 28, note 3, is placed over rest in this measure. M. 47, C, flat for e' of m. 48, note 1, placed between notes 1 and 2 in this measure; T, flat for e' of m. 49, note 1, placed over rest. M. 52, C, "ta" is adopted from Peterhouse; sharp canceling the flat of m. 48, note 1, precedes note 2 in this measure. M. 66, B, the flat before e, note 2 in m. 62, has not been canceled; introduction of the flat before the e in m. 67, note 1, indicates the e in m. 66 is to be sung natural. Mm. 70–72, B, the flat before e, m. 67, note 1, has not been canceled for the two remaining Es on the staff, m. 70, note 4, and m. 72, note 1, both of which should be sung natural. M. 85, B, the flat before e, m. 76, note 1, has not been canceled; the e, note 1, m. 85, should be sung natural to avoid dissonance with the contratenor b-natural as notated in the MS. M. 86, C, underlaying of the text is not clear; the sharp of m. 85, note 1, has not been canceled; but the intent surely is for the signature flat to be back in effect. Mm. 88–90, S, "privaris" is not set. M. 98, S, the musica ficta sharps for notes 4 and 5 are given because mm. 96–98 recall mm. 21–23, where the c″ is sharped in the MS. M. 105, all voices, ₵. Mm. 133–34, B, in Peterhouse "Elizabeth" is repeated on the textless notes of Lambeth. Mm. 135–36, T, "Elizabeth" is inscribed in large letters. M. 137, B, note is an erroneous semibreve, editorially emended according to St. John's. M. 157, no change in the meter takes place, but metrical signs are notated for the third opening of the MS; that for the B is lacking; T shows ₵; in Scone an ornamental "N" at the beginning of each staff; the text in T opens "Nunc vine," in all other voices "vine." Mm. 173–84, S, the sharp before f″ in m. 173 is not subsequently canceled on this staff (the staff extends through m. 184, note 1);

the Fs in mm. 176–83 should be sung natural; a sharp following note 1 of m. 184 prepares the singer for the sharp introduced at the beginning of the new staff, m. 184, note 2. M. 182, all voices, "inmundum." M. 184, note 2, S, new staff through m. 200—the sharp preceding note 2 is not subsequently canceled on this staff, thus the Fs of m. 192, notes 2 and 3, should be sung natural and the Fs of m. 189, note 1, and m. 196, note 2, may be sung natural or sharp. M. 191, note 3, Md, the sharp of m. 189, note 2, has not been canceled, but the context of the text and music indicates that the signature flat is back in effect.

Acknowledgments

The editor wishes to thank the librarians of Lambeth Palace Library, Gonville and Caius College Library, The Bodleian Library, Peterhouse Library, St. John's College Library, Cambridge University Library, St. Michael's College Library, The National Library of Scotland, and The British Museum for providing microfilms and photostats and for permission to examine the manuscripts. Particular thanks are extended to Lambeth Palace Library for permission to print the facsimiles from the Lambeth Choirbook.

An expression of special gratitude is extended to Flora Elizabeth Reynolds and Susan Summerfield, my colleagues at Mills College; to Father John R. Keating, S. J., of the Jesuit School of Theology at Berkeley and of the Graduate Theological Union; to Nathan Rubin of California State University, Hayward; and to Martha Henninger Rubin.

Margaret Lyon

Notes

1. As translated by Oliver Strunk, *Source Readings in Music History* (New York, 1950), 195. Strunk translates *jubilare* (to jubilate) as "to shout," but Frank Ll. Harrison prefers "to sing in a florid manner," *The New Oxford History of Music* (London, 1960), 3:303, n. 2. Albert Seay suggests "to improvise melodically" and *cantare* "to compose." See Johannes Tinctoris, *Proportions in Music (Proportionale musices)*, trans. Albert Seay, Colorado College Music Press Translations, no. 10 (Colorado Springs, 1979).

2. Harrison, *The New Oxford History* 3:303–4.

3. Frank Ll. Harrison, *Music in Medieval Britain*, 2d ed. (London, 1963).

4. Gustave Reese, *Music in the Renaissance*, rev. ed. (New York, 1959), 775.

5. Jeffery Pulver, "Robert Fayrfax," *Musical News* (20 January 1917): 35; W. H. Grattan Flood, *Early Tudor Composers* (London, 1925), 38.

6. Denis Stevens, "Prime Musician of the Nation," *The Listener* (21 March 1957): 493.

7. *The New Grove Dictionary of Music and Musicians*, s.v. "Fayrfax, Robert," by Nicholas Sandon.

8. In French, *Camp du drap d'or*, so-called for the display of wealth and splendor that marked the pomp and festivities at the meeting in France between the two kings June 4 to 24 at a place between Guines and Ardres.

9. To qualify for a music degree at Oxford and Cambridge the composition of a Marian mass, or in some instances a mass and an antiphon to the Virgin, were required. See Frank Ll. Harrison, ed., *The Eton Choirbook: I*, Musica Britannica, vol. 10 (London, 1956), xiv.

10. *Robert Fayrfax. Collected Works*, ed. Edwin B. Warren, 3 vols. (Rome, 1959–66).

11. See Frank Ll. Harrison, "The Eton Choirbook, Its Background and Contents," *Annales musicologiques* 1 (1953): 150–75, for an explanation of the latest date for the writing of the main part of the manuscript. The three works are published in Frank Ll. Harrison, ed., *The Eton Choirbook*, Musica Britannica, vols. 11–12 (London, 1956–61): *Salve regina* in 77:32; *Ave lumen gratiae* in 12:146; and the Magnificat *"Regale"* (edited from the Lambeth source) in 12:96.

12. Harrison, *Music in Medieval Britain*, 164.

13. As quoted by Edwin B. Warren, *Life and Works of Robert Fayrfax*, Musicological Studies and Documents, vol. 22 (1969), 23.

14. In The National Library of Scotland, MS Adv. 5.1.15, at Edinburgh, and in Cambridge University Library, MS Dd. xiii.27 (contratenor), the opening words of the second line, "Te laudat," are reversed to read "Laudat te" in all voices.

15. R. Alec Harman, ed., *Thomas Morley, A Plain and Easy Introduction to Practical Music* (London, 1952), 331–32.

16. Pulver, "Robert Fayrfax," 35.

17. See the diagrams of three antiphons from the Eton Choirbook in Harrison, *Music in Medieval Britain*, 316.

18. Ibid., 251.

19. Andrew Hughes and Margaret Bent, eds., *The Old Hall Manuscript*, 3 vols., Corpus Mensurabilis Musicae 46 (American Institute of Musicology, 1969–73). See No. 83, a Credo by Leonel Power, and No. 18, a Gloria by Byttering. Both works are in three-part counterpoint. In Power's Credo different portions of the text are given to two different voice parts, to be sung over a textless third part; in Byttering's Gloria different portions of the text are superimposed as double texts for a treble part, the voices singing simultaneously in melodic unison two different portions of the text over a textless tenor and contratenor.

20. Harrison, *Music in Medieval Britain*, 255, and Denis Stevens, *Tudor Church Music* (London, 1961), 25.

21. See *The New Grove Dictionary of Music and Musicians*, s.v., "Faburden," by Brian Trowell. According to Trowell, the term faburden, ca. 1460, designated a technique practiced in England for improvising on a plainsong. But originally, 1430 or earlier, it was the name given the lowest sounding part in this improvisatory technique. This faburden part was sung a third below the plainsong (a fifth below at the beginning or close of a word or

phrases) upon which it was improvised and which it paralleled. Another part was improvised above the plainsong moving parallel to it at the interval of a fourth. The result was a note-against-note progression of three parts (the plainsong was in the middle) in which the plainsong was harmonized as a series of 6/3 chords with an occasional sound of the octave and fifth. Slight ornamentation might occur at the ends of phrases in order to permit suspensions at the cadence.

The role of faburden as cantus firmus in the history of the polyphonic setting of the Magnificat in the fifteenth century in England was established by Frank Ll. Harrison when he identified as faburdens to the Magnificat Tones a set of mensural monophonies in British Museum, MS Royal Appendix 56, an organ book of ca. 1525. These monophonic melodies were inscribed with text and arranged as a series according to the eight Magnificat Tones with their different endings. They were intended as faburdens upon which the organist improvised the even-numbered verses of the Magnificat in alternation with the chanting of the odd-numbered verses on the Magnificat Tone. The instrumental improvisation by the organist replaced polyphonic vocal settings of the even-numbered verses.

Harrison not only identified these melodies as a set of faburdens but also recognized them as a source for the recurrent material common to the tenors in Magnificats in the Eton, Lambeth, and Caius Choirbooks. Thus, he was able to demonstrate that in settings of the Magnificat in fifteenth-century England polyphonic verses were, with few exceptions, composed on a faburden to the Tone, not on the Tone itself. According to Harrison this use of an elaboration of a chant as cantus firmus is peculiar to the Magnificat. See Frank Ll. Harrison, "Faburden in Practice," *Musica disciplina* 16 (1962): 11–34 and idem, *Music in Medieval Britain*, 348–49.

22. Paul Doe, ed., *Early Tudor Magnificats: I*, vol. 4 of Early English Church Music, (London, 1962), viii.

23. For an extensive study of these practices and the choral foundations, see Harrison, *Music in Medieval Britain* and idem, "The Eton Choirbook, Its Background and Contents."

24. Harrison, ed., *The Eton Choirbook*.

25. The Mass *O bone Jesu*, which lacks a cantus firmus and in which the movements are linked only by a motto, is an early example of a derived or parody mass. The Magnificat *O bone Jesu*, in which the cantus firmus is a faburden to the Magnificat Tone VII, shows in a few instances a relationship to the Mass *O bone Jesu*. But with only the one voice of the antiphon known, it is not possible to establish completely the exact nature or the extent of the relationship of these three works.

26. Harrison, ed., *The Eton Choirbook: I*, 72, 108, 116.

27. Sandon, "Fayrfax, Robert," 444.

28. Dom Anselm Hughes, "An Introduction to Fayrfax," *Musica disciplina* 6 (1952): 101.

29. Gloria V of the *Liber usualis* (Desclée: Tournai, 1961) is the fifth Gloria in the Sarum Gradual; Gloria III is the first Gloria in the Sarum Gradual. Walter H. Frere, ed., *Graduale sarisburiense* (London, 1894), plates 12* and 9*, respectively.

30. Warren, *Life and Works*, 112.

31. Thurston Dart, *The Interpretation of Music* (New York, 1963), 148.

32. Harrison, *Music in Medieval Britain*, 324–25.

33. Hughes, "An Introduction to Fayrfax," 91.

34. *The New Grove Dictionary of Music and Musicians*, s.v. "Sources: MSS," by Charles Hamm and Jerry Call.

35. Sturton or Stourton, fl. early sixteenth century, is perhaps William Sturton of the Chapel Royal in 1503 and 1509–10; in the Eton Choirbook the surname "Edmundus" has been added in a later hand. (See *The New Grove Dictionary of Music and Musicians*, s.v. "Sturton.")

36. Andrew Hughes, "Mensural Polyphony for Choir in 15th-Century England," *Journal of the American Musicological Society* 19 (1966): 352–369. This is a study of the manuscripts and of the music and liturgical practices in England as sources for an understanding of the process whereby the performance of polyphony (during the medieval period sung by soloists) was gradually taken over by a chorus in the early fifteenth century. Hughes focuses primarily upon the Old Hall Manuscript (dated ca. 1420) but includes, as well, consideration of English manuscripts from the end of the century, particularly the Eton Choirbook. The scribe's use of red ink in the Old Hall Manuscript for duets that alternate with sections of three or more parts in certain chanson-style settings is considered analogous to the designation "unus" and "duo" in the duets in Italian manuscripts of the time. In English sources as well as in Italian, Hughes states, the scribe's intent is to indicate performance by one voice to a part in contrast to choral performance. And when a scribe in the second half of the fifteenth century uses red ink (as in the Eton Choirbook, where it is employed throughout in sections for a reduced number of parts), he concludes, the intent is the same, to signal performance by one voice to a part in contrast to choral performance.

For a discussion of the Italian sources see Manfred F. Bukofzer, "The Beginnings of Choral Polyphony," chapter 5 of *Studies in Medieval and Renaissance Music* (New York, 1950).

37. Walter Lambe, b. ?1450–51; d. after Michaelmas 1499. (See *The New Grove Dictionary of Music and Musicians*, s.v. "Lambe, Walter," by Nicholas Sandon.)

38. Walter H. Frere, ed., *The Use of Sarum* (Cambridge, 1898–1901), 2: Appendix. Sarum is the Latin name for Salisbury in England, where, at the cathedral church, there developed a rite (called a "use," therefore, "Sarum use" or "use of Sarum") that spread throughout England. Although other rites evolved at such great religious centers as York and Hereford, it was the rite at Salisbury that governed English religious practices. The Sarum use differed in certain respects from that at Rome, as did the plainsong melodies, which exhibit recognizable melodic characteristics peculiar to Sarum. The Sarum use prevailed throughout the Middle Ages and until 1547, when, at the time of the Reformation, it was removed.

39. Harrison, ed., *The Eton Choirbook: I*, xx.

40. See Roger Bray, "The Interpretation of Musica Ficta in English Music, c. 1490–1550," *Proceedings of the Royal Musical Association* 97 (1970–71): 29–45, and Paul Doe's reply, "Another View of Musica Ficta in Tudor Music," *Proceedings of the Royal Musical Association* 98 (1971–72): 113–22.

41. Harrison in *The Eton Choirbook: III*, 167, identifies this antiphon as the "third antiphon at Lauds on the Nativity (September 8) and Conception (December 8) of the B.V.M." The editors of *The Old Hall Manuscript* described the chant as "also used separately for the devotion of the B.V.M." (A. Hughes and M. Bent, eds., *The Old Hall Manuscript*, 3:24).

Text and Translation

Since translations of the mass and the Magnificat texts are widely available, a translation is given here of only the votive antiphon *Aeterne laudis lilium*. The translation has been made by Flora Elizabeth Reynolds.

Aeterne laudis lilium

Aeterne laudis lilium O dulcis Maria,
Te laudat vox angelica, nutrix Christi pia;
Jure prolis gloriae datur harmonia,
Salus nostrae memoriae omni agonia.

Ave radix, flos virginum, O sanctificata,
Benedicta in utero materno creata
Eras sancta puerpera et inviolata,
Tuo ex Jesu filio, virgo peramata.

Honestis caeli precibus virgo veneraris,
Regis excelsi filii visu jocundaris:
Ejus divino lumine tu nusquam privaris,
Gaude sole splendidior virgo singularis.

Isachar quoque Nazaphat necnon Ismaria
Nati ex Jesse stipite qua venit Maria;
Atque Maria Cleophae, sancto Zacharia,
A quo patre, Elizabeth, matre Sophonia,

Natus est Dei gratia Johannes Baptista,
Gaudebat clauso Domino in matrice cista.
Lineae ex hoc genere est evangelista
Johannes. Annae filia ex Maria ista

Est Jesus Dei Filius natus in hunc mundum,
Cujus cruoris tumulo mundatur immundum.
Conferat nos in gaudium in aevum jocundum,
Qui cum Patre et Spiritu Sancto regnat in unum.
Amen.

Lily of eternal praise, O sweet Mary,
The angel voice praises you, pious nurse of Christ;
Let a song be duly given to the glory of your child,
Deliverance from every suffering in our memory.

Hail, O sainted root, flower of virgins,
Created blessed in your mother's womb,
You were the sacred and inviolate mother,
Maiden most beloved by your son Jesus.

Virgin, you are venerated in noble, heavenly prayers;
At the sight of your son, the high king, you rejoice:
Of his divine light you are never deprived,
Rejoice, matchless Virgin, more splendid than the sun.

Isachar and Nazaphat as well as Ismaria
[Were] born of Jesse's stock from which came Mary;
And Mary of Cleopha [and] blessed Zachary,
By that father [and] Elizabeth, Sophonia [her] mother,

Was born, by the grace of God, John the Baptist.
He rejoiced in the master hidden in the mother's womb.
Of this line is the evangelist
John. Of that Mary, Anne's daughter,

Jesus, the Son of God, was born into this world,
By whose bloody tomb the unclean is cleansed.
May he unite us in bliss for an eternity of joy,
Who reigns together with the Father and the Holy Spirit.
Amen.

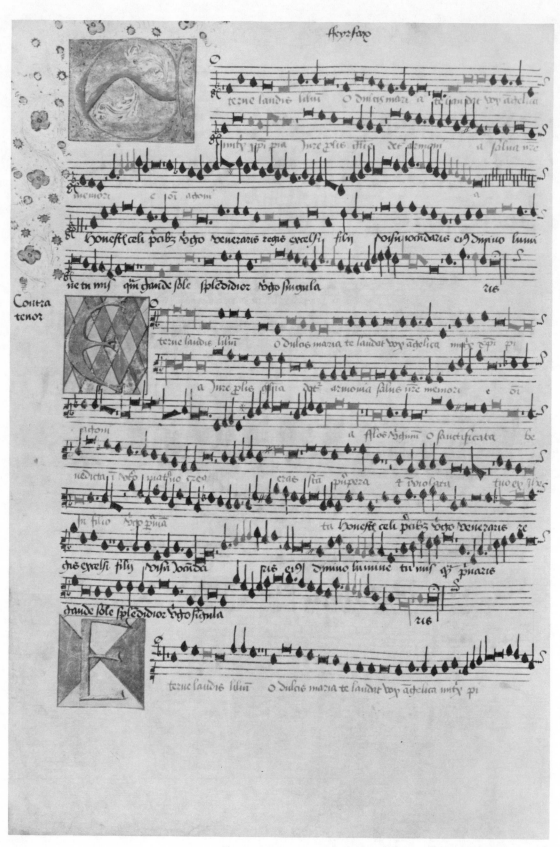

Plate I. *Aeterne laudis lilium*, first opening.
London, Lambeth Palace, MS 1, fol. 56v. Original size: 67 x 46.8 cm.
(Courtesy Lambeth Palace Library)

Plate II. *Aeterne laudis lilium,* recto of first opening.
London, Lambeth Palace, MS 1, fol. 57r. Original size: 67 x 46.8 cm.
(Courtesy Lambeth Palace Library)

SACRED MUSIC
FROM THE
LAMBETH CHOIRBOOK

Mass *Regali ex progenie*

Gloria

6

9

Credo

16

20

de- scen- dit de _____ cae- - lis.

- dit de ____ cae- - lis.

- dit de ____ cae- - - lis.

- tem⟩ de cae- lis.

- dit de cae- - lis.

Et in- car- - na- tus _____

Et in- car- na- tus _____

Et in- car- na- tus _____

_____ est de Spi- ri- tu _____ San-

_____ est de Spi- ri- tu San- -

est _____ de Spi- ri- tu _____ San- -

Sanctus

125

- di-

130

42

Agnus Dei

49

qui tol- lis___ pec- ca-

-i,

-i,

-i, qui tol- lis pec- ca-

52

Magnificat *"Regale"*

*Plainsong on Tone VIII for the odd-numbered verses has been supplied from the Sarum Tonale in *The Use of Sarum*, ed. Walter H. Frere (1901), Appendix, ii.

III

Qui- a re- spe- xit hu- mi- li- ta- tem an- cil- lae su- ae:

ec- ce e- nim ex hoc be- a- tam me di- cent o- mnes ge- ne- ra- ti- o- nes.

IV

[Superius]

Qui-

[Medius]

[Contratenor]

[Tenor]

Qui- *a*

[Bassus]

Qui-

-a *fe-* *-cit* *mi-*

-a *fe-* *-cit* *mi-*

fe- *-cit* *mi- hi*

ctum _____

ctum ____ - no-

ctum _____ no-

no- men _____ e-

men

men _____ e-

jus.

jus.

e- jus.

jus.

V

Et mi- se- ri- cor- di- a e- jus a pro- ge- ni- e ___ in ___ pro- ge- ni- es ti- men- ti- bus e- um.

VI

bos men- te _____

bos _____ men-

men- te _____

men- te _____

cor- dis _____ su- i.

-te _____ cor- dis _____ su- i.

cor- dis _____ su- i.

cor- dis _____ su- i.

cor- dis su- i.

VII

De- po- su- it po- ten- tes _____ de se- de, et ex- al- ta- vit hu- mi- les.

VIII

IX

Su- sce- pit Is- ra- el pu- e- rum su- um, re- cor- da- tus mi- se- ri- cor- di- ae su- ae.

X

[Contratenor]

Sic-

[Tenor]

Sic-

[Bassus]

Sic- ut lo-

- ut lo- cu- tus est ad pa-

- ut lo- cu- tus est ad pa- tres no-

- cu- tus

175

ham et se- mi- ni e-

ham et se- mi- ni e-

ham et se- mi-

180

jus in sae-

jus in sae-

ni e-

185

cu-

jus in sae- cu-

190

cu- la.

la.

la.

XI

Glo- ri- a Pa- tri, et Fi- li- o, et Spi- ri- tu- i San- cto.

XII

68

Aeterne laudis lilium

[Superius]

105

I- sa- char quo- que ____ Na- za- phat nec- non Is-

Contratenor

I- sa- char quo- que ____ Na- za- phat nec- non Is- ma-

110

-ma- ri- a ____ Na- ti ex

-ri- a Na- ti

115

Jes- se sti- pi- te qua_ ve- nit Ma- ri-

ex Jes- se sti- pi- te qua_ ve- nit Ma- ri-

120

125

82

DATE DUE

HIGHSMITH 45-220